SOCA BABY

For the entire soca community:
the lovers of soca, the children of soca,
the artists, DJs, producers, and all the
carnival chasers.

And a special thank you to Ras Shorty I

This book was inspired by our children and the sweet melody of soca.

Soca Baby
Text copyright ©2023 by Ariful Mowla + Qef Johnson
Illustration copyright ©2023 by 18/1 Graphics Studio

First Published in Brooklyn, NY, USA by Water Lily Publishing
ISBN: 979-8-9903099-0-6
Library of Congress Control Number: 2024906209
www.waterlilypublishing.com

Ariful Mowla   Qef Johnson

SOCA BABY

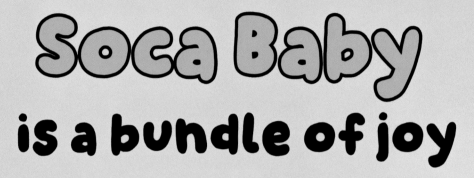

Soca Baby

is a bundle of joy

Born to parents who

LOVE SOCA, oh boy!

Soca Baby

loves **BRIGHT** colors

WEARS A
ONESIE AND BACKPACK

LIKE NO OTHER

and spreads

HAPPY CHEER

Soca Baby's
laughter rings out

LOUD and **CLEAR**

Soca Baby
loves to sing
Sings to the beat

and drums on
EVERYTHING

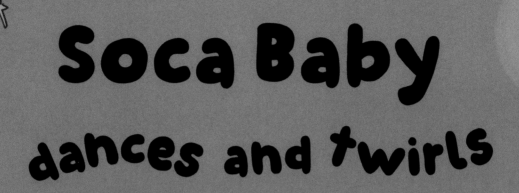

Soca Baby

dances and twirls

Soca Baby moves in soca swirls

soca's Caribbean roots
with sunshine, beaches
and tropical fruits

Soca Baby
knows how to play

From sunrise
to sunset
EVERYDAY

Soca Baby's
spirit is sweet
and FREE

a little
WARRIOR
full of energy

the love for LIFE
Soca Baby will never hide

Soca Baby
you're one of a kind

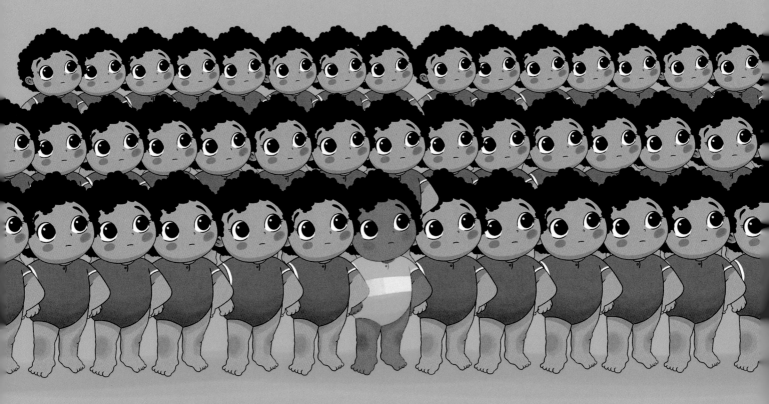

Your love for soca
will be forever enshrined

Soca Baby

keep shining bright

You're a true

SOCA STAR

in every right!

Made in United States
Orlando, FL
16 December 2024